HIC! HIC! HIC! HIC! HIC! HIC! HIC! HIC! HIC! HIC! HIC! HIC! HIC! HIC! HIC! HIC! HIC! HIC! HIC! HIC! HIC! HIC! HIC! HIC! HIC! HIC! HIC! HIC! HIC!

Copyright © 2012 Mike Herrod
BalloonToons® is a registered
trademark of Harriet Ziefert, Inc.
All rights reserved/CIP data is available.
Published in the United States 2012 by
🍎 Blue Apple Books
515 Valley Street, Maplewood, NJ 07040
www.blueapplebooks.com

First Edition
Printed in China 09/12
HC ISBN: 978-1-60905-255-3
2 4 6 8 10 9 7 5 3 1

HICCUPS ON THE BUS

HIC!

YIKES, JAMIE!!

OH NO! NOT ON THE DAY OF MY BIG PLAY!

I WILL CURE YOU! THE SHOW MUST GO ON. FOR I, JENNA, AM THE BIG STAR!

AND I AM IN BIG TROUBLE. HIC!

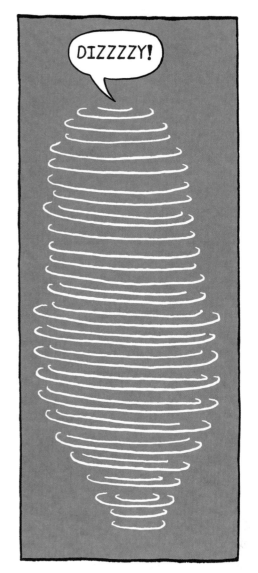

THE HICCUP WORKOUT

COACH BLOAT, WE NEED YOUR HELP!

WAIT, DON'T TELL ME! I'M GREAT AT GUESSING.

HIC!

HIC! HIC!

YOUR DOG ATE YOUR GYM SHORTS.

HIC!

HIC!

HIC! HIC! HIC!

THE BASKETBALLS ARE TOO ROUND.

HIC!

HIC!

HIC!

HIC! HIC!

THERE'S BALONEY IN YOUR TENNIS SHOES.

HIC!

HIC!

OH NO. MY STARRING MOMENT WILL BE RUINED.

AND LOOK AT THAT CROWD! HIC!

WOWZA!!

WE DID IT! AND I WAS THE BIG STAR! I'M SO EXCITED! HIC! HIC! UH-OH...

HIC! HIC! HIC! HIC! HIC! HIC! HIC! HIC! HIC! HIC! HI HIC!

OH-NO! HIC! NOW I HAVE THE HICCUPS. BUT AT LEAST WE KNOW THE CURE!

WAIT, STOP! I HAVE ANOTHER IDEA...

to be continued . . .